The Berenstain Bears®

HELP AROUND THE HOUSE

Stan & Jan Berenstain

GT
PUBLISHING

The Bear family lived in a tree house down a sunny dirt road deep in Bear Country.

It was a big handsome tree house where the members of the Bear family — Mama, Papa, Sister, and Brother — lived very happily.

"The cubs are right, my dear," said Papa. "There's such a thing as being too neat and clean. Why don't you relax and just let things slide?"

Then one day Mama looked at the dust,

and the messy bathroom,

and the things that
needed to be put away,

and decided to take Papa's advice.
She decided to relax and just let
things slide.

She stopped dusting. She stopped scrubbing. She stopped putting things away. For a while that suited Papa and the cubs just fine.

Oh, the dust got up
their noses and made them
sneeze a little.

AHH CHOO !

And the wet towels
began to pile up in the
bathroom.

And the clutter really wasn't that much of a problem. Except for the time Papa slipped on a roller skate and fell down the stairs.

Papa and the cubs had
never seen Mama so relaxed.

But Papa and the cubs weren't relaxed at all.
There were armies of dust devils gathering under the
furniture.

The bathroom — well, the less said about the bathroom the better!

And the clutter had gone from bad to worse.

Then one night, when the dust was rising and the bathroom had gotten really messy and the clutter was so thick you could hardly walk, Papa had a dream. He dreamed the dust devils had joined together and turned into a giant dust monster and chased him around the house.

Brother had a dream, too. He dreamed the bathroom had turned into a scary jungle.

Sister had a dream, too. She dreamed the clutter of toys had come to life and was attacking her.

Papa woke up shouting "Help!" The cubs came running in, shouting "Help!" They all told Mama their dreams.

"Well," said Mama. "I had a dream, too. My dream was that we would all pitch in and share the dusting, the scrubbing, and the putting away."

And that's what happened. The Bears not only
lived happily in the big tree house down a sunny dirt
road deep in Bear Country, they lived happily ever after.